SAVING THEM

UNLEASHING HELL BOOK THREE

VIOLA TEMPEST

**Saving Them
Unleashing Hell Book Three**

Cover Design by Burning Phoenix Covers

CONTENTS

SAVING THEM

VIOLA TEMPEST

CHAPTER 1
BELLA NOVA'S POV

THE CLOCK ON THE WALL IS THE LOUDEST THING I have ever heard, and I'm counting the ticks like the gun that had gone off when I killed Brick.

Tick. Tock. Tick. Tock.

Dr. Schultz is waiting for me to say something, but I don't know where to start. I'm wearing an oversized sweater to cover up the mark that he'd left. I still don't know what had come over me. I like to think I'm not one to ask based on emotion. I like to think that I can do an okay job of thinking about consequences, considering the logic of things. But my track record isn't looking great.

Schultz taps his pen against his notebook, waiting.

Draven? I whisper it into my brain. I try it on the left side; I try it on the right. I try it in the front, and I try it in the back. I try to say his name through my body, sending it down to my toes. It's impossible to know when he's around. But I think I've figured out his kryptonite.

"I'm worried," I finally say between the tapping of the pen and the ticking of the clock. I can't focus, can't search my body for him until I *can* focus.

The pen clicking stops.

Draven?

"Be more specific. About whom, dear? About what? When did it start?"

I noticed it a day or two ago. The kryptonite, not the worry. It made as much sense as something could when you're grasping at straws. Draven gets weaker—loses his hold on me—when I think of sunshine. He's a demon, so maybe it all adds up.

However, thinking of sunshine isn't enough when someone is already inside your head. It feels like whenever I begin to contemplate the warmth of a summer day, imagine the blinding light that one might see from staring straight into the sun, he's slamming down a brick wall. Now I *am* the sunshine. I have, discreetly, rubbed my arms and the back of my neck with the essence of lemon.

My sweater is yellow. I'm wearing a sun ring on the finger next to my pentagram ring, another one of the many pieces of jewelry mother had given me from her odd collection.

For now, I think Draven is at bay.

"About me," I finally say. Schultz raises an eyebrow but doesn't say anything else. He wants me to explain. "I've been... feeling unlike myself."

He shifts in his seat. "Tell me more."

"Well," I sigh, crossing one leg over the other, "I've been... making rash decisions. I've been distrustful, yet too trusting all at once. I'd say I'm paranoid, maybe. I've been... having these nightmares."

"You mentioned those last time." Schultz nods his head as if he already knows. He scribbles a few things down. "It may help if you give me specifics, Ms. Nova."

I take a deep breath. What instance can I tell him without making me seem insane? How can I sound just insane enough so that he gives me advice, a prescription, but doesn't admit me into a hospital?

Should I be going to a hospital?

I hate myself for thinking of Stephanie. I can't even figure out the right answer, think critically about whether or not I need to go stay somewhere for a while to get my mental health in order. Rumors would get around. And Stephanie will win.

"Like... with Daven," I try to explain. Schultz leans forward, peers at me over his glasses, but doesn't add anything. "Is it okay if I talk about him?"

He lets out a slight professional chuckle as he sits back against his chair. "Why wouldn't it be?"

"Well, aren't his family members clients of yours? I don't want to offend—"

"I'm a doctor, Bella," he interrupts me, setting his notebook on the side table next to him. "I can't disclose to them anything you say. I have no favorites. They're a lovely family, but trust that anything you say is between you and I."

"Okay," I mumble, sitting up. "I guess I can give you an example. With Daven."

"Sure," he nods.

"We broke up." I feel a sadness in my chest, though I'm usually more angry than sad. "And... I don't know if it's my fault or not."

"Explore that. Talk about that more."

"Something happened." I scratch the back of my neck, hoping that breaking the surface of my skin will allow the essence of lemon to hide me from Draven. "With this girl at school. She hates me, and she embarrassed me, and I... could have communicated with him better about it. But I just... felt like everything was.... like it had all been a part of this big conspiracy to hurt me."

"The paranoia." Schultz nods, taking the notebook and scribbling again. "That's a common thing for many mental... dilemmas."

I notice him not trying to say ill. I don't care if he says I'm mentally ill. I almost want him to—maybe that means I just need a bowl of chicken soup, a little rest, and a cold compress pressed to the front of my skull to freeze Draven out.

"Sure," I mumble again, shifting in my seat. "Sure. Yeah, maybe it was silly of me to think that Daven could have anything to do with what Stephanie did—"

"And what did she do?" He crosses one leg over his knee and peers over his glasses again. I take another deep breath. Does he feel like a dentist? Pulling teeth?

"At the homecoming dance—the one Daven took me to—she... ugh. It was awful! I don't even want to talk about it. She humiliated me in front of the whole school."

"And you think Daven helped?"

"No, of course not."

"So, why were you upset with him? Walk me through that thought process. Tell me what you were thinking when you decided you didn't want to communicate in the way that you—as you have mentioned—thought would be successful."

I shrug. "I guess there was a... voice in my head."

He perks his eyebrows up. "A voice—"

"Not a real one!" I jump in quickly, and we both smile. "Sorry, I'm new to therapy."

"Everyone is at one point. And that's okay. Tell me what you want to tell me, and I will respect your privacy. When I'm asking these questions, Bella," he smiles when says my name, refers to me as a friend, "it's to guide you to a different understanding of what you have already said. Yes?"

I shake my head yes and continue. "There was a

little voice in my head, an itch, that said if Daven really cared about me, he would have chased after me. And made sure I was alright. This happened less than a week ago, and he's already dating someone new. And I know it's because *I* am already dating someone new, but—"

"Let's pause here." Dr. Schultz puts his pen and notepad back down on the coffee table, grabs his coffee mug, and leans forward before taking a sip. "You're already dating someone new? And this only happened a week ago?"

Draven? I whisper it again and hear nothing. But how am I supposed to know if he's just hiding somewhere, watching over me, waiting to hear what I say about him? I'm careful about my word choice. I don't want to know what might happen if Draven gets angry.

"He was there for me when Daven wasn't. He has this... energy. It's like a magnetic connection. I don't know how to explain it."

"Do you feel this way a lot?" he asks. I feel as though it's a trick question.

I quickly answer, "No!"

But maybe I do. Maybe I've felt these magnetic, fatal attractions to others for whatever reason. What about Brick? What about Daven? And Draven?

I'm looking down at my fingernails, picking at the acrylics I got for the homecoming dance. They're beginning to lose their shine, and there's a gap between the nail and my cuticle. Daven had paid for me to get them done.

When I look back up at Schultz, he's smirking. "It seems like you're thinking about your answer a little more critically now."

I deflate, leaning my head against the cushion of the old couch. The lighting in here is relaxing to some, I'm sure, but it isn't to me. He has lamps, not fluorescents. The lamps are on their lowest setting, making mostly everything cast an eerie shadow. *Draven?* But none of the shadows transform. I am relieved, and still suspicious, and still paranoid, all at once.

"I guess I do feel like I fall for people pretty fast."

He nods. "Do you think it's healthy for you to jump back into something so quickly after Daven?"

I shrug. "You're supposed to tell me."

"How was your relationship with Daven, Bella? Was it... safe?"

I scrunch my eyebrows, tilting my head back. "Safe? What do you mean?"

"Well, if I can be blunt," he explains, "it's pretty peculiar for a client to come to me about their significant other unless it's couples' counseling. Except for, of course, if the significant other is worried their partner will say something they shouldn't."

"What do you mean?"

"How'd you get that mark on your wrist, Bella?"

I look down. Just barely, the mark that Draven had left on me is peeking out.

"Oh," I pull down my sleeve self-consciously, "that wasn't Daven. Daven was nothing but respectful toward me."

"Okay," he sits back, "I just want to make sure this wasn't an... abusive situation. I was hoping he hadn't forced you into not telling me the whole truth."

"No, he would never do that."

"So, *is* that the whole truth?"

The clock is ticking so loudly. Shadows are shooting across the room as he moves, always forward and back, and forward and back, the shadow of his pen projecting across the wall. I feel highly anxious; I feel sweaty! What *is* the whole truth?

"I think I'm seeing things. And no one else seems to see them. Not... not *real* things. I'm just—paranoid, Dr. Schultz. And anxious. And I feel like there's two of me. Not that I have a split personality or anything like that—but there's a version of me that makes great decisions, plans things out, and then there's another version me that just takes these leaps that don't end up going right in the long run."

He nods. "This sounds like, at least from our first conversation, a case of Bipolar Disorder. I think you are manic when you're making these big, leaping decisions, Bella. And those with Bipolar Disorder—"

"I have Bipolar Disorder?" I repeat as a question. I try to think of what I know about Bipolar Disorder, and this just doesn't fit. "I'm not having mood swings, though."

"That's a common misconception," he explains. "Most people with Bipolar Disorder swing between mania and depression. The mania is sometimes glorious highs of making wild decisions—selling everything you own and moving to a convent, quitting your job without notice for no good reason, purchasing several instruments though you've never played. And then comes the depression. The loneliness, the exhaustion."

"Hm," I whisper. That's all I can say.

"Those who are bipolar may jump into relationships. They may have an intensity. And their intensity may become reflected by others, especially those who also have something going on."

"So, what's the cure?"

"No cures here," he said, scribbling. "You'll have to take medication, continue seeing me, and work at making adjustments. In time, it's a truly controllable disorder, especially in your case. It seems to be mild. Let's try you out on some mood stabilizers and see if they help. You can come back to see me in a week."

He's already handing me a script from his pad, with a funny name written across it in bad handwriting.

"But... what if I don't have Bipolar Disorder?"

"Then the pills probably won't help, but they won't hurt you, either. Let's go ahead and schedule our next appointment for next week." He moves from his armchair and goes over to his desk, looking through his calendar. "Same time? Same day?"

I look at the word again. I can't even make out all the letters, and I pray that a pharmacist will be able to.

"Would Bipolar Disorder give me hallucinations?"

I ask. It sounds abrupt coming out of my mouth. I sound scared, though I don't mean to.

He whips his head around, face in a poorly disguised horror. "Bella, are you having hallucinations?"

I shake my head rapidly. "No. I was just asking. Same time, same day, next week."

I get up quickly, grabbing my purse, and I bolt out the door.

CHAPTER 2
BELLA NOVA'S POV

Draven is waiting, sitting on my bed when I return home. I'm happy to see him here. If he's here, then he wasn't at my appointment. I ditch my essence of lemon into my purse before hanging it up on the back of my door, sliding next to him on the bed. I slide my hand into his.

"How was the... dentist?" he asks. He doesn't understand what a dentist is, in the same way he doesn't understand what a street taco is or why one might purchase a car. I put the new bottle of pills I picked up at the pharmacy on my dresser.

"I have a cavity," I lie, leaning my head onto his shoulder.

"Is that what those are for?" he asks, nodding his head toward the pill bottle. "Those are very bright. Can you put them away?"

With this, I confirm my suspicions. He doesn't like yellow. He doesn't like orange. Anything that reminds me of sunshine makes him feel sick. Without speaking, I get up and grab my pills. I open up my sock drawer and put them at the bottom, covering them up with the socks. Dr. Schultz made it clear that I don't need my parents to consent to my treatment, and I'm not even sure how they'd feel about it.

I don't think of my parents as anti-mental health in general, but before I went to Schultz, I did a lot of self-reflection. I thought about PTSD, about my childhood, about my upbringing. Mom and dad were always great supporters and advocates for us—but had it been *us?* Or had it only been Ace, who was always getting into trouble at school and constantly smoking pot in his room?

Mom was always hovering, but she did it in the smartest way possible. She didn't tell me I couldn't do things or accuse me of this and that—instead, she weaseled her information through kindness. And once she figured out what she wanted to know, it seemed like the solution was a conversation between her and dad. But I wasn't in on those conversations.

Then, things mysteriously seemed to solve themselves.

Like in the third grade. I was in a class above my grade level because I was doing so well, and funding cuts had just taken the gifted and talented program away. There was a teacher's assistant, who was a high school or college associate or *something* to that extent, who had taken a special interest in me.

I don't even remember her name anymore, because things got shut down just like that. A snap of a finger. She had helped me research these folktales, had encouraged me to learn more about them, and I had let it slip to mom. Quite honestly, as interested and excited as I was about the stories, they were making it impossible for me to sleep. I was having horrific night-mares, I was losing my appetite, and I was getting these dark circles under my eyes. Mom found out and snapped. I never saw that girl again.

"You're looking more and more human by the minute," I tell Draven, giving him a once-over. He's wearing an old pair of Ace's jeans and one of his hood-ies. His nails, which used to be long and black, have been painted over with a neutral shade and clipped just enough to make him look more normal.

His skin has a healthy glow, thanks to my mother's foundation and my fathers "secret" concealer. He almost looks human if I avoid staring at him for too long. And no one else would. Something about his demon state makes him only half-visible at any given moment.

He's like something in your peripheral vision. When he isn't focused on you, you're not focused on him. He wouldn't jump or scare you if you did start to notice, either.

I wonder if it's an evolutionary tactic on our part. If one were to notice a demon and be frightened by it, it would just feed them more. It would just make the demon stronger. I've noticed the way my negative emotions exponentially grow when I'm around Draven: anger, fear, resentment, sadness, *guilt*. And I've noticed how he feeds on it.

"It seems like I'll need to look the part in order to save my family," he says. He is suspicious as he watches me from across the room. "I don't like your garment."

"Okay," I reply, simply taking it off and putting it in the laundry basket. Underneath, I'm wearing a black and purple tank top with stripes on it.

"I love that color!" he cheers, smiling mischievously.

"Black?" I laugh. "Not surprising."

He shakes his head. "The other one."

"Purple?"

"Purple. Yes, I know what it's called. I've just been going mad here. It's so different compared to where I'm from." He gets off the bed and closes the distance between us, putting his hands on my hips. I give him a soft smile but look away. "What is it?"

"I'm just tired, and my teeth hurt," I lie. I climb onto the bed and crawl under the top sheet, the one too small for him to fit under. *Regret.* Regret and guilt are exemplified through my bones right now, through my breathing. It feels like all I am is regret and guilt. I no longer feel human at all. I'm now closer to what Draven is; I know this for sure.

"What did they do to you, my sweet?"

I want to cringe at the word, but I don't.

"Can you go over the plan with me again?" I ask quietly.

"We will save my family," he says.

"But how? What do I have to do?"

He sighs, sitting on the edge of the bed. "Have I done something wrong, Bella?"

I feel a tear coming out of the corner of my eye. I try not to sniffle. The sadness is magnified now.

"How do I even know you're real?"

"Because I'm right here."

"That doesn't mean anything. The human brain can create hallucinations. It can create sounds and noises and feelings. This could all be a fucking halluci-nation. How *humiliating*. How freaky. I'm a freak!"

I say all of these things out loud, though I have spoken them in my head since the first time I met Draven. And it's true that Draven, since that day, has been nothing but kind to me. But this just gets weirder and weirder, and I think I've gone past the point of no return.

If I'd been honest about the hallucinations the first time around, would I be enjoying normal high-school girl things right now? Or would I still be here, on my bed, in an ever-flowing river of sadness and anger and fear, speaking to a demonic creature that may or may not even be real?

"You *want* to be crazy," he tells me. Getting off the bed, he goes to the corner and into my sock drawer. I don't even stop him. He moves my socks around until he finds the bottle.

"These aren't for your teeth; I'm willing to stake everything on it. I'm going to ask your brother."

He goes toward the door.

"Why would I *want* to be crazy?" I ask. He stops in his tracks and looks over his shoulder.

"Being crazy would be easier than believing in demons. It would be easier than accepting that you are the Chosen One, that many may die at your hands, and it'll be for a justice you refuse to understand."

He moves through the door stealthily, turning into a shadow as he crawls toward my brother's room. Ace is high, that I know for sure—it smells like a skunk in my bedroom because the window is open, and he likes to blow smoke out the window. What he doesn't know is that the wind usually blows it at me. I shake my head, getting up to light a candle, and lie back down.

My phone buzzes. It's Daven.

Can we talk?

I shake my head as though he can see me, and then I put my phone inside my bedside table drawer. I can hear it buzz a few more times, but I don't want to look. I don't care to look. Any chance of reconciliation that Daven and I had ended when he and Stephanie started dating. And you know what?

I open up my bedside table drawer again and grab both a pen and a sheet of paper. I write down, for Dr. Schultz, more thoughts. I don't want to forget all of this next week.

Why would Daven date Stephanie unless he was in on the prank? I write. *Maybe I'm not paranoid. Maybe I'm just gaslighting myself.*

I'm proud of myself for using the word "gaslighting," a word I'd found during my research. Bipolar Disorder hadn't come up a single time, but psychosis had. If I were in psychosis, wouldn't Ace be, too? He could see Draven. Most people could.

What worries me is that psychosis doesn't have to mean things just popping up out of the air as hallucinations. It could mean seeing something, something that was really real, and your mind twisting the image. It could distort it to have a brand-new meaning, to make their words sound different, to make your understanding of them different.

Kind of like when you dream, and you're at school with no shoes on, but so is everyone else, and your youth pastor is there. And your dog that died when you were seven is teaching the class, and it all just makes sense because your dream brain makes you *think* this is reality. What if that's what I'm doing with Draven? What if he's just some man who found me on the street, who's been stalking me, and now lives in my room?

Draven returns with the pill bottle.

"A mood stabilizer?" he asks. "To make your moods more... consistent?"

I nod. He hasn't gone into the muck of why I want to use them—because I'm crazy, and I'm scared.

"Yes," I mutter quietly, pulling the blanket up to my chin.

He sits on the bed, frowning. "Oh, Bella. I'm sorry. Demons tend to have this effect on people. No wonder you seem so sad."

"What effect?"

"Every negative emotion you've ever had in your life is going to be heightened around me. I thought that since you're the Chosen One, it would be different. But I was wrong. It sounds like it happens even *worse* for you. I'll turn it off."

"Turn it off?"

"Yes."

"You can just do that?"

"Sure," he says. "For you, I will. Just a matter of thinking about it."

I smile a little, hopeful that he's right, and my moods might stabilize on their own. But why then, has this happened to me my entire life, even before Draven? I push this thought out. Draven will solve this problem. Maybe it never existed before him. If I can be happy again, calm, I'll stop worrying about the past.

"I'm sorry for being so distant," I whisper to him. And I mean it.

I was all over Draven the day before. I was all over Draven the day before that. And I've been all over

Draven since we slept together. Today's swing in the other direction *must* have been prompted by his demonic traits, not by me. And he's not doing all this on purpose.

He crawls under the tiny blanket with me and gives me a kiss on top of my forehead, repeating the same sentiment that he's repeated to me a hundred times since we met.

"I've been waiting over five millennia to meet a girl like you, Bella Nova."

CHAPTER 3
DAVEN PORTER'S POV

My heart stops when I see Bella at school. Not in the way it usually does—usually when I see her, I feel my hands get a little clammy, and I can feel my forehead start to sweat. She's made me feel like a babbling idiot, not the calm and collected person I used to be around women.

Stephanie, though she does have beauty in her own way, doesn't make me nervous at all. Bella, the most beautiful girl I've ever seen in *her* own way, makes me buckle at the knees.

But today, when I see her, it's not her beauty or my regret or my promise (the promise I haven't promised her yet for the fear that it will compromise this mission: *I PROMISE I will not let Stephanie get away with this*) that shakes me. It's the boy she's holding hands with.

There's something off about him. Not just that he's holding hands with my beloved. I'll admit that I *am* jealous of him, and that may be skewing my perception. But it feels as though he walks around with this aura of superiority, maturity, and understanding of the world that guys my age just don't really have.

He's here, at the high school, and he's wearing jeans and a hoodie. His face looks smooth, wrinkle-free. And his skin is actually flawless! He doesn't look a day older than seventeen—though he does have a unique way about him—but he does just *seem* older.

They both walk past me, Bella flipping her hair and smiling while the guy gives me a look that sends my stomach to my feet. I feel almost dizzy after seeing him. It's as if he's looking at me to say he's going to rip me from limb to limb.

But no, I'm crazy to think that; it was just a look! In fact, as soon as he walks past me, I take my hand off of Stephanie's shoulder—which I've been longing to do since I put it on her—and run to the restroom. I puke, and I puke *violently*. I didn't eat much this morning. And I wouldn't ever buy Stephanie a bagel or get her a coffee like I had for Bella.

But it feels like when I start, I cannot stop.

"You alright man?"

"I feel like I'm about to throw up my intestines," I say between pukes, and I mean it jokingly, but it probably sounds serious with the way I'm gagging.

"Want me to get the nurse, man?"

I can only half make out the voice, but I see a pair of canvas sneakers. They're signed by *Walker Walking*, a local indie band that Michael and I went to see last summer. He had them sign his shoes because his band tee was already filled up with signatures.

"Michael?" I ask.

"It's me," he replies. "I saw you running in here."

Michael and I haven't exactly been on speaking terms since the homecoming dance. He, for reasons I can't relate to, has a huge crush on Stephanie. He has since we were in the fourth grade. Even though she has a rotten heart and is cruel and unkind, he likes her. I guess everyone deserves love at the end of the day.

But if me dating her ruins her for him, I'd be happy with that, too. Michael deserves better.

"I must have food poisoning or something," I mutter to him, saliva dripping out as I speak.

"Nah." Michael lets out a breath. "You just saw Bella with that weirdo. You're sick with jealousy. I know the feeling."

I feel a pang of guilt in my chest. *I know the feeling.* I had been so caught up in my anger and wanting to help Bella that I honestly hadn't thought of Michael for a second. It was only after I had already concocted my plan and gotten one foot into it that I even remembered Michael.

I open up the stall.

"Hey," I say to him.

"You look as pale as a fucking ghost," he says curtly, his curly hair bouncing as he shakes his head, "and I can't say I feel bad about it. You kinda deserve it, man."

"I'm the world's biggest asshole, aren't I?"

"Yeah."

And I'm smiling, but he doesn't laugh. He means it.

I sigh. "What if I told you I don't have feelings for Stephanie?"

Michael raises an eyebrow. "I'd say that dating her right in front of me—*and* Bella—is a pretty weird way of showing it."

I go over to the sink and splash some cold water on my face. When I look up at the mirror, I see that I really am as pale as a sheet of paper. How much should I tell Michael?

"Did you see what Stephanie did at the dance? To Bella?"

"What?" he asks, leaning against the pillar that separates the stalls. "What Stephanie did to Bella? What dance?"

I give my face a gentle slap and reach for the water bottle in my backpack. I finish the whole thing in one gulp, and I'm starting to feel a little better. The water bottle is actually a gift from Bella, before she was even my girlfriend. It's yellow, with a little sun printed on it.

"She humiliated her, man. She had this box, this weird ass box that sprayed her with all this gross stuff and—it was so mean, Michael. Stephanie is *awful*. I don't understand why you like her at all."

Michael seems to be considering this, but then speaks quickly in defense. "It's really hard for me to listen to you and take you seriously when you're literally *dating* her, Daven."

"I just want her to admit what she did to Bella. I want the full confession. If I can figure out how she did it, place her there, and get her to—I don't know, record her saying she did it, or even *texts* saying she did it—they will probably expel her. The school has a zero-tolerance bullying policy."

Michael raises his eyebrows. "You want her expelled?"

"Shh!" I hiss at him, looking toward the door. "I haven't even told Bella I'm doing this. She'd probably tell me not to or say she can fight her own battles—"

"So... maybe you shouldn't, and maybe she *can* fight her own battles."

"Do you think what Stephanie did was right?"

Michael is quiet. He shakes his head *no*. "She can be... intense."

"And you can still date her when she goes to the school across town." I splash my face with water again. "But Bella's life will be so much easier if Stephanie isn't here. And not *just* Bella. All the girls in our grade would celebrate. They'd play *Ding Dong! The Witch is Dead* on the announcements—"

"Watch it," Michael smiles, "I like Stephanie."

I turn to him. "But you shouldn't. You deserve better."

Michael looks down at his feet, frowning. "Maybe I do."

"Can I count on you?"

He looks up again. "Count on me for what?"

"Can I count on you to keep this a secret between us?"

He shakes his head. "Daven, I don't think you're thinking straight. Can you imagine what this might look like to Bella? She's already dating that weirdo. I think you doing this will make her go insane."

"It'll be worth it in the end," I reply, going toward the door. "I know it. Can I count on you?"

Michael takes in a deep breath, then shakes his head *yes*. I leave the restroom and go back toward my locker, where Stephanie is still leaning and twisting her hair. It'll all be worth it in the end.

I know it.

CHAPTER 4
DRAVEN ASMODEUS' POV

Bella is shaken from seeing Stephanie and Daven together, which angers me more than I had originally thought. I want to crawl under his skin, take his soul right from his body, and watch as his eyes melt out of his head, but I know I'd lose Bella if I did that. Instead, I give him a punch to the gut from the inside out. I can hear him puking as Bella and I walk away.

Now, with no interest in her classes when my family is at stake, like the good girl she is, we're sitting on a park bench near her school. Her spirits are much higher than they were the night before, when she came home with the pills.

We didn't have anything like that in my day. Sometimes you'd eat the powder from crushed up herbs, and those would help you with some basic things, such as breaking a fever or throwing up poison. But the only remedies we had for the brain were the ones that opened a layer to the other dimension, where you could look at it through a magnifying glass. And even then, those were better consumed whole than in powder form. Those were my favorites.

"I want to help you," she says to me.

I can see fear in her eyes. As a demon, this is something I crave. But not with Bella. I don't want her to feel a negative emotion in her entire life, especially if it's one I have caused.

Bella is like a mirror. The chosen ones often are. It can lead them through a life of great sadness and anger. Like the entire world is out to get them, and it only gets worse the more resentful and hopeless they feel. Many of the chosen ones don't survive.

But sometimes the Chosen One is met with manifestations of happiness and luck. These ones don't last long, either. Because their riches always lead to something that will eventually break them. Maybe drugs, maybe worse. And once the descent happens, it happens quickly.

From what I can tell, Bella's family has done well for themselves because they request little and expect less. I have suspicions about the mother, however, about the pots of herbs she simmers as she cooks, and the salt she pours at her door.

But as far as I can tell, Bella has never heard a word from her mother about their involvement in the Underworld. About their chosen status. That makes her the perfect victim—but I am weak. I pray that her and I can work together. That I don't have to turn her in in order to get what I want.

So, I begin with a sob story. Maybe it's manipulation. But I'm a demon. There's much worse I can do.

"Your family reminds me of mine. You'd do anything to save them if they were in trouble, wouldn't you?"

She doesn't need to think about it. She nods. "Of course, I would."

"Because they'd do anything to save you, right? Even if you'd done something wrong?"

I can see a flashback swim across her eyes.

Yes, I know about Brick. I can feel her shame. I can see the scene written across her skin because it constantly eats at her. I'll use this to my advantage, without ever letting her know that I know.

She looks down at her hands, which are wrapped in mine as we sit at a picnic table near her school. "They would."

I nod. "Well. I did something wrong. When I was young. I was your age, probably. Maybe younger."

I was the exact same age, actually, that she was when she killed Brick.

"What'd you do?" she asks, eyes wide and innocent.

"I opened a door. It doesn't sound bad, but we had many warnings in our village. Humans in your generation call them *folktales*, but they were as real to us as the weather. We knew of demons who would rise to the surface, like weevils in rice, every thousand years. And it was time. So, we had new laws to follow," I tell her. "All doors remain open. All bodies of water are to be ignored. Don't look inside trees with holes."

"Those sound silly." She smiles. I love the way she lightens things with her smile.

"Yes, I thought so, too. They were hard rules to follow because they didn't make much logical sense. So, I ignored the most important one, *don't go swimming in the river at night*. The demons just needed a little of my life source to rise. And then... I let them take my father. The demons. I thought that would be enough for them. But then they came back for the rest of us and half the village."

"Because you went swimming? Draven, that's an innocent mistake. Not even a mistake! I don't know what I'd call it!"

I shrug. "It's a mistake that cost my family and I several millennia, and many of those were spent in horrendous pain and unbearable torture."

"Why did you give them your father?"

I try to think of a good answer.

"I thought they would stop with just him."

"Why did you think that?"

"They said they would."

"And they didn't?"

I sigh. "Demons lie. It's our favorite thing to do. We lie to anyone we can lie to. We lie when we're telling stories; we lie when we're telling secrets. We just *lie*."

Bella raises an eyebrow. "Do you lie to me?"

"You would know, Chosen One."

This answer satisfies her.

"Are they still being tortured?"

That's a loaded question. How might one define *torture?*

I nod. "They are."

She nods, too, as if she's made a decision. "Why me?"

I shrug. "I don't know why you were chosen. But you were."

"And what exactly am I supposed to do? Go to Lucifer's throne and beg for your family's release?"

I shake my head. "It's a little more complicated than that."

I hope to keep the secrets of its complication.

"Well, I need more information." Finally, she seems a little irritated. I know she's not stupid, and she knows I'm hiding, avoiding the real conversation. I feel her irritation itchy under my skin, the frustration thrusting itself under my skull.

"Okay. Well, first, we will try to find a portal. The Chosen One is supposed to be able to open it."

"Like you? Are you a chosen one?"

I shake my head. "That was different. That was

when the layers between the portal were already thin. They aren't so thin right now."

"Well, I've never seen a portal. I don't know what it's supposed to look like."

"It's not like that. It'll be an element, a fire or water or earth or spirit or—"

"A spirit?"

"Like a place of worship. A place of prayer that you feel connected to."

She frowns, scratching in between her brows with one of her long-painted fingernails. "Yeah, religion and I haven't mixed well. I don't go to church."

"Unsurprising. Churches tell only lies. You probably know it's all bullshit."

She chuckles, still not looking up at me. "Maybe. I don't think my family has ever stepped foot inside a church."

"Maybe your mother knows." She snaps her head up, anger in her eyes, pushing past her mild irritation and growing full force.

"Don't say that."

I pretend to act surprised, as if I'm not actively trying to push her buttons. "Sorry, I didn't mean to offend you."

She softens.

"I just hope that if my mom knew, she would've told me. It feels like a pretty big thing to not tell your own daughter."

"Yes. Especially because it can mean so much danger, so much pain. You'd want to warn your child what might be coming for them, so that they could be safe. So, they wouldn't have to protect themselves."

I can see the guilt dancing across her skin again. If I can drive a wedge between her and her mother, her and her purest human connection, I might be able to convince her that what we have to do is warranted.

"You love your mom?" she asks.

"Of course, I do. And it's my fault that she's stuck down there."

"What kind of torture is she facing?"

Another truth I cannot tell. My mother is actually doing a lot of the torturing. After being asked for thousands of years if she was ready to succumb to the darkness, she finally agreed.

"Things I don't want to tell you, Bella. I don't want you to be scared to go down there."

"But then you are no better than my mom," she says sharply. "You don't want me to be protected or safe. I need all the information that I can get in order to be safe and protected."

I stifle a smile. My plan is working as expected. "I thought your mother doesn't know."

She looks back down at her nails. "She didn't. She *doesn't*. I just meant—"

"I will tell you all you need to know to be safe. We will find a portal. That part will be hard, not because it'll be hard to find, but because getting through the door isn't pleasant."

"How do you do it?"

"With a key. But the key is you. It's the worst thing

you've ever done. The most horrendous thing that's ever happened to you. It'll play it back for you in the mirror, and if you can face yourself, if you can still push through, then you're in."

"That's what I'm worried about. What if I don't?"

I sigh. "You will get through it. We all do."

She rests her head on my shoulder, looking out at the rest of the park. The peaceful scenery in front of us. Swans swimming in the pond, trees blowing in the wind. This will all be madness soon enough.

"When do we start?" she asks.

"Now." I take her hand and guide her up, and we walk toward the thick trees of the forest. I can feel it all rushing through me now, a wild energy. This is working. It's finally going to work!

When my mother and sister join us up here, will they have a thirst for torture and pain? It has truly become an acquired taste of ours all those years down there.

And what if the door remains open?

Many will die. Bella's family may be amongst them, her friends.

Is lying to her worth my family coming back to me?

Save us, Draven! Help!

They feel my wavering heart. Okay, it's worth it.

CHAPTER 5
BELLA NOVA'S POV

Draven leads me toward the forest. I've been at this park very few times before. My mother said that during her childhood, this park was best known for tarantulas, hawks, and scorpions. For this reason, I avoided it like the plague. I wonder now what was true and what was a lie.

The trees are hanging low, and there is a break where five tree stumps sit in a circle. Draven looks at me, noticing my ring.

"You need to take that off," he says.

I clutch my hand defensively. "No way! My mom gave it to me."

Sure, I'm angry with her, but I would never take this ring off. That's what she told me when she gave it to me—never take it off.

He sighs, annoyed. "We cannot get through unless you take it off."

It's a pentagram, which would send many Christians clutching at their pearls. I'm confused and livid—there is so much to know, and I fear that Draven will only tell me the parts that are convenient to him.

"I thought pentagrams are like demonic signs or something. Don't they have something to do with the devil?"

Draven huffs, rolling his eyes. "No, Bella. It's quite the opposite, actually. The witches of your Earth are essential to keeping the demons *away*. The pentagram helps with that."

"Well, then why can you hold my hand? Why are you here?"

"It's not like throwing salt at a snail, Bella. Yours doesn't even look charged."

"Then why do I have to take it off?"

His lips tighten into a straight line.

"Obviously, no demon would wear a pentagram. If the demons see you, if they notice you, then they will crawl under your toenails and shoot out of your eyeballs."

My stomach turns. "What the fuck? That's sick!"

"Take the ring off, and you won't have to worry about it," he tells me.

I don't know if I believe him, but I'm too far in it now to say anything else. I take the ring off slowly. There's a low hanging branch, and I slip it on, giggling to myself about how it feels like I'm proposing to the tree.

A sadness then overwhelms me.

How silly! A teenage girl thinking about marriage as I descend into Hell.

I feel as though I've put myself in a spot that makes the future impossible, hopeless. I won't have a ring on my finger one day. I won't have a wedding, or be a bride, or have babies. I'll have to live with all of these mistakes I've made, with knowing that I've walked through the valleys of Hell.

Draven leads me toward the stumps, bringing me closer to the middle. Beetles are crawling all over the ground. It makes my skin crawl.

"Ew," I say, crinkling my nose. He lets a breath out, laughing.

"Yeah, maybe to you."

He stomps his foot, and the beetles scurry away. He then extends his hand toward me, and I follow his lead, both of us standing in the small space between the stumps.

"So... what now?"

He takes his hand, making it into a fist, and I cannot believe it. He crouches down really low and knocks. That's all, just knocks. He looks up at me. "Think you can do that?"

I roll my eyes. I wonder how many times I've almost, accidentally, fell into the depths of the Underworld because I was randomly knocking on things. I crouch down and give it one, two, three knocks.

In the blink of an eye, I'm in a dark and squishy room. It's like my nightmares all over again. The floor feels like it's made of jelly, like I could inadvertently sink through it at any given moment.

It's a deep purple down here, like an eggplant. The walls are shiny. I'm scared, but I'm also not surprised, given that I've been here before.

"Oh," I mumble to myself quietly. The sound echoes off the walls, which are made of the same substance.

"Get ready," he says, and all my emotions swarm over me at once. I'm feeling all the shame, all the guilt, and all the regret as I see his image projected onto the shiny purple wall, now solid and thick like glass. Like a mirror.

I see Brick, first as a baby coming out of his mother. Then, I watch as he grows up. He's a kid who doesn't seem to play well with others. But he's adorable, nonetheless, a child. I watch as his father and mother beat him mercilessly. I watch as he beats his girlfriends, or any woman who gets near him, mercilessly.

And I see as he kills his victims, ties them up, and assaults them. I see him chugging bottle after bottle of whiskey, throwing the glass at the wall and cutting his own hands and feet on the shards, sweeping them up, and looking at them confused the next morning.

And things get even weirder at one point. Suddenly, in these images of him drinking the dark liquor from glass bottles, there are more and more shadows in the room. They are looking over him. Trying to grab at him, trying to jump into him. And finally, one succeeds.

"Draven!" Someone is calling. "Save us!"

"Keep going, Bella! We're so close!"

Then there's me.

"Draven? Is that you?"

It's the sing-song voice of a little girl.

"I'm coming, Melanesia. Get ready!"

"Please, help!"

"Push, Bella! Don't waver! Don't succumb to the fear! Show that you are worthy!"

I'm watching it all happen, now through his eyes. Through the eyes of Brick, who was a broken child skipped over by the adults who were supposed to take care of him. I watch as he hurt other girls just like me.

And now, from his eyes, the eyes of a predatory demon. I'm watching this half-Brick, half-demon getting ready to pluck me like a chicken. The first time he saw me and... every detail. All of it. I'm disgusted just watching the stupidity. Like a lamb to the slaughter. I'm vulnerable and easy to take, and I would've been taken by this demon, forced to do something that Draven has been kindly guiding me into.

And I want to do this for him, but we're getting to

the end of the scene and... and *the end*. I shriek. I can't do it. I can't watch!

In the blink of an eye, we're back inside the forest.

Draven is red with fury, and I'm gasping for air.

"Water!" I cough. "I need some water!"

I point toward my backpack, which I had ditched near my ring, begging on my knees for Draven to grab the yellow water bottle hanging out of the pocket. He's livid as he stomps over to the bag, kicking it in the opposite direction. I bring my hands to my throat.

"What the fuck, Bella? You were almost there! Why did you stop?"

I point to my throat again, shocked that he kicked the bag. "Please! Water!"

My voice is hoarse. I feel sunburnt. I feel dizzy. I feel *nauseous*.

"I could hear my mother! I could hear my sister! Look what you've done! Now they're still in there, being tortured! And what if a guardian overheard them?! What if someone knows the veil is now thin and comes to kill me?"

"Draven!" I try again. My voice is nearly gone now.

He rolls his eyes, stomps over to the bag again, grabs the water bottle, and throws it at me. I open it quickly and lap at the water desperately. I fall back onto the ground, and a few stray beetles crawl toward my fingers. I jump up, and then the sun reflects off my ring.

But Draven sees where my eyes have gone and goes toward it, grabbing the ring from the tree.

"Why did you do that?" he demands again.

"Draven, give me that. It's mine!"

"My family is mine. And you stole them."

"I didn't steal anything!"

"You're the only one who can get them back, and you *refuse* to help!"

"I didn't refuse, Draven!" I scream at him. "That was my first fucking time in the depths of Hell, having to watch something so horrifying, something I've worked desperately to erase from my memory. Not to mention that you *didn't mention* that demons have been trying to get me for years!"

Draven is silent. Then he rolls his eyes, walking toward the park. "Fucking duh, Bella. You need to figure some shit out before we try this again. I don't think you understand any of this."

He's too far gone for me to say anything to him.

"Then help me understand," I whisper to myself. Because it's abundantly clear that Draven is hiding something.

CHAPTER 6
DAVEN PORTER'S POV

Bella hasn't been in any of her classes today.

But I know she was at school. One, I saw her this morning. Two, she left something in my locker.

We exchanged combinations before we even started dating. She lost her Literary Composition textbook, and we'd been sharing the same one ever since. She would put it in there after she took the class, first period, then I'd grab it for fourth period.

Somewhere in between when I'd put my geography book back at the end of yesterday, and this morning when I took out my math textbook for my first period class, she had put a yellow rain jacket in my locker with a little note.

This is for CeCe. I heard her asking your mom for one.

There was a tiny duck embroidered on the pocket. It was shiny, the rubber vinyl material making squeaky noises as I observed it. I put it straight into my backpack before Stephanie could see.

Normally, I'd leave her alone, let her have the independence she deserves. But that's if I hadn't seen her with that freak this morning. I don't trust him. And though I fell for Bella quickly, she fell for me quickly, too. I worry about her, which is ironic. I don't worry about myself because I know that what I felt was real. But how could she have known, said it back to me so quickly?

When I finally spot Bella, she has her backpack flung over her shoulder, and she is quickly walking toward the library at school. She has a twig in her hair, and she looks like she's been crying. I want to reach out to her, but Stephanie swoops in out of nowhere.

"So, *babe*, should I come over later? I'd love to meet Jackie."

"Jackie?" I roll my eyes, "My mom?"

"Duh, Madame Mayor!" Stephanie is popping and chewing a piece of gum, and it disgusts me.

"Why?" I'm laughing because Stephanie has a thousand and one surprises. You'd think one or two of them would be, at least, good surprises. But none of them have been thus far. I look back toward the library, and Bella is gone. I sigh, defeated.

"Just wanna see what it's like living a life of luxury," she says, reaching her hand toward my left thigh. I smack it away. She huffs. "What? I'm your girlfriend now."

"I never said that," I hiss at her, going toward my locker. "We're dating, but I never said that."

"Why are you like this, Daven?" She chases after me, then leans against the locker next to mine. "What's your problem? You don't still have feelings for her, right?"

"No, of course not," I lie through my teeth, though I say it sarcastically. Then an idea comes to me. I discreetly take my phone out from my pocket and put it into my locker, hitting the recording app. I then press the record button and shut the locker. "Not after what you did to her."

Stephanie raises an eyebrow. "You think it was me?"

"I *know* it was you," I say with a fake enthusiastic tone. "That was so funny! How did you come up with that? How did you get everything to explode out of it? It hit Bella right in the face. How?"

She smirks. "I just had some nerds from the rocket club help. They powered it up, basically made it into a bomb. I just had to tell Bella that it's my way of saying sorry—"

I'm almost too angry to conceal my feelings, but I

press on. My face tightens, and I can see Stephanie watching the rage cross my face. "You? Sorry?"

"She wouldn't have opened it otherwise, duh!"

I pause, taking another deep breath.

"Okay. Who else helped you?"

"I'm actually, like, really smart, Daven. I just needed the nerds to draw up the plans, and I did everything else myself. You should've seen her face when it hit her. You only got to see the aftermath of my conniving work."

"Wow," is all I say back. Wow is actually an understatement. This girl is truly *evil*.

The bell rings, and Stephanie looks up, giving me another smile. "Gotta go! See you later?"

"Sure," I mutter. I watch as she walks away, going up the stairs toward her Spanish class. Then I open my locker again and grab my phone, ending the recording. "Evil bitch."

I shove the phone into my pocket and head toward the principal's office.

But that's when I see him.

Hunched over as he walks, his feet drag toward the entrance of the school. He looks nefarious in his manner alone. The energy he exudes is equal parts intimidating and mystifying.

The principal's office can wait.

I throw my backpack over one shoulder and wait until there's a large enough distance between us, then I follow him. I sneak behind pillars as we exit the school, and eventually, I lurk behind trees as we go toward the nearby park.

Why is he going to the park?

If I hadn't seen Bella go into the library, I'd be worried that he'd buried her out there. This guy is *that* weird, *that* creepy. Instead, I see him head toward the creek.

I stand behind a tree, about twenty-five feet away. I'm careful to not make a sound.

Draven reaches down, grabs a handful of water, and throws it into the air.

And I'm shocked! The water freezes, mid-air.

"I need to speak with Melanesia," he says to the frozen water.

"What did you do to deserve Hell?" a bellowing voice asks.

"Show me my sins!" Draven says back in an annoyed tone. He says it casually, as enthusiastically as one might say, "Check my account balance" or "Connect me to customer service."

Quietly, I creep closer. The water has spread itself thin, displaying a larger-than-life version of a scene. It's Draven, but he's wearing clothes that someone might've worn centuries ago. It's a smock, with a sword on his hip. And he's using a smaller knife to cut something.

As I look closer, I see what that something is. It's a boy, who looks just like him. His eyes are blackened, his body nearly blue. Draven is carving symbols all over his body. I see it, too, from the perspective of the body. Then I listen as the water vision of Draven speaks.

"I sacrifice thee to Lucifer in exchange for riches and food."

I throw my hands over my mouth.

"Where are you?" a new voice asks. I see on the screen a little girl. She can't be much older than CeCe. But she looks eerie, a little off. I can't quite make out what it is about her, not from this far away.

"I'm going to be there soon. Prepare yourselves."

"How are you going to get here?" the little girl asks again.

"I have found the Chosen One, Melanesia."

Melanesia? That must be her name.

"Mother grows weaker," Melanesia whispers.

"Where is your father?"

"Away. Trying to figure out how to get up there like you did. He is furious about your departure, brother."

Brother?

"He can come up here whenever he wants. I don't care. I just want you two spared. I want you two up here." Draven tenses his brows as he continues to speak, like he's worried about something.

"He is thirsty for the blood of the humans."

"There is plenty of that up here. For now, I am only bringing the Chosen One to get you and mother. Do not tell your father."

"And what if I do, brother?"

"Then I will have the Chosen One banish you

right back to the Underworld, and you will have to suffer down there without mother and I."

"My father is a royal man. I will not suffer," Melanesia protests.

"You *will* suffer without your mother. Even you know that."

"He will just come up to the surface and bring her back."

"He cannot come up to the surface now, not without the Chosen One." Draven seems awfully confident in his words.

"And you trust that I won't turn her over?"

"I don't trust you as far as I can throw you, Melanesia."

"So, why do you come to save me from Hell, brother?"

"Because I sacrificed a brother once to meet Lucifer. Now I will sacrifice a lover to fix my mistake." Draven lowers his head, a sense of shame washing over him.

A lover?

I take a step back. And a tree branch breaks.

"Will I like it up there, brother?"

"Hello?" Draven looks back into the forest, then back at the water. "An animal. Yes, sister, you will love it. Trust me. Please."

"Though you don't trust me?"

"Yes."

"Fine. Hurry."

"Don't tell your father."

"I won't."

And then the water drops down into the river. I turn around and run. As my feet finally hit asphalt, a car just starting up from the stop sign hits me. It's not moving fast, and I'm not in too much pain, but I hit my head against the hood of the car.

What did I just witness?

CHAPTER 7
BELLA NOVA'S POV

I can't stop seeing it.

I regret, immensely, having agreed to do anything with Draven. And still, I wonder if Draven is even real.

"Is it possible that... I mean, can we talk more about hallucinations?"

Dr. Schultz nods, taking a sip of his coffee and putting his pen down.

"Ms. Nova... I think I do need to acknowledge the irregularity of this circumstance. Are you struggling with the medication? With the current dosage? I do have flexibility in my schedule for instances like this, but I wasn't expecting to see you until next week."

I scratch an itch behind my neck.

I can't stop seeing it.

Lamb to a slaughter, lamb to a slaughter, lamb to a slaughter. And so many times in my life, I *was* the lamb to a slaughter. There are so many things becoming abundantly clear to me as I think about it more. That teacher's assistant that my mom had gotten fired—was she also a demon, possessed? Are female demons gentler?

And what about the other boys? What about all the strange instances in my life, where strangers got a bit too close or waiters lingered a bit too long, and my mom barked or snapped or pulled me up by the elbow to lead me away? Were they also just demons trying to get something from me?

What do they want?

Except I'm worried that I *do* know what they want. Draven has made it clear that he wants his family released from the Underworld, but the research I did at the library a few hours ago doesn't make it seem that simple.

Portals are easy to get through once they're open. For millennia, people have been sent to the depths of Hell. They're packed in there, like sardines in a can, ready to burst out of the first open portal. How did Draven even get out without more people escaping? How had the other demons?

There are some things they know that we don't. They, the demons that is, know the workarounds that humans cannot understand. They know, too, the politics of Hell. The way they must please their lord, Lucifer.

But do they know what we know? Do they know about how we use pentagrams for protection, how yellow and color and florals and happiness are their kryptonite, how a little essence of lemon may drive them mad? Do they know this? Are they prepared for it?

I'm pedaling through these thoughts, and Schultz is still looking at me, head tilted. He wants me to answer him. But I don't know how.

Because even through all this research and all these realizations, I'm hoping with my entire being that this is all just a manifestation of my guilt. That I've only broken through my own consciousness and gone into psychosis because I just feel *awful* for killing Brick. I'm hoping that I created this demon thing, this whole story, just to make everything make sense.

I'm hoping I'm just insane.

"I just needed someone to talk to. Maybe the pills aren't working."

Schultz nods. "Okay. Tell me how you have been feeling over the past few days."

How I've been feeling? It's less about how I feel and more about where I've been, what I've seen. Me, through the eyes of a man who intended to kill me—to do much worse, quite frankly.

"I had... a bad experience in my past."

He nods again. "I've noticed some signs of a possible past trauma. A complex version of this can often be mixed up with Bipolar Disorder."

"Sure, well... I was this way before it happened. But this didn't help, of course."

He shifts his weight, crossing his legs. "Do you want to tell me more about this experience, Bella?"

Don't tell him anything, Bella.

I gulp. Draven is here. When did he come back? Where is he?

Schultz doesn't move an inch. He's still waiting for my answer.

He'll lock you up. If you say a word, he will lock you up. Not in the loony bin, Bella. In jail. In prison. He has to tell on you if you did something that hurt someone else. You killed someone, Bella. You're on the run. Do not say a word.

I turn my head, looking behind me. It sounds like he's right behind me, whispering into my neck. I can feel his breath. But there's no one there.

"Bella?" Schultz asks as I look back and forth frantically.

I'm breaking out into a cold sweat. I can feel the beads dripping down the front of my head.

"I'm hearing things..."

Stop, Bella.

Schultz doesn't say anything for a moment. I reach toward my bag, grabbing the little vial of lemon essence from the front pocket. I find the lip and pour out a few drops onto the top of my hand. Then I take my index finger and rub it on the back of my neck, the top of my forehead, the corner of my eyes, and the center of my wrists.

What are you—?

His voice grows quieter.

"Are you hearing things right now, Bella?" Schultz asks.

"Not anymore," I respond, holding the vial up. "This helps."

He smiles. "What helps, Bella? What is the voice saying? Is it in the room, or is it in your head?"

"Both. He's in the room, and he's in my head, if I can be honest with you. He's everywhere. I can only get rid of him with this."

"What is it?" he asks again. "May I see it?"

And I hand him the bottle. He gives it a little sniff.

"It's an oil."

"Lemon," he says, "is that correct?"

I nod my head. "It helps. Yellow helps. Flowers help. Feeling happy helps. Thinking happy thoughts and having happy memories help."

Schultz is quiet again. He leans back against his chair, wondering. I see him look toward the phone on his desk. If he has to admit me, fine. I hope he does.

"Bella, how long have you been hearing this voice?"

"Since the nightmares began."

"And when did the nightmares begin?"

"When we moved."

"And when did you move?"

"When the bad thing happened." At this point, I'm whispering. Not because I want to, but because I'm running out of steam. I'm running out of energy. I'm going to cry soon, and I'm going to completely break down. Everything that I've tried to shove down, everything that I've ignored, everything that I've numbed... they're all here at the surface.

I've made some awful decisions. I've made some big mistakes. And whether Draven is real or not, I'm being punished for them. I pray that this punishment is one of my own creations. I pray that Draven isn't actually real.

"What do you think we should do about this, Bella?" he asks.

"Can you send me somewhere?"

"Yes."

"I see him, too. I see things, Dr. Schultz. I'm seeing things and hearing things."

"We can find a safe place for you. I'm going to call your parents, but first, I'm going to call my assistant." Schultz gets up and goes toward his desk. His shadow jumps against the wall, the lamp illuminating him. But his shadow straightens, stands tall though he hunches. Then Schultz looks back at me. He throws the glass vial of lemon essence onto the ground. His eyes are completely black.

"Doctor—"

"Bella, why aren't you listening to me?" he asks. It is Draven's voice.

"What are you doing? Are you hurting him?"

"Of course not, Bella. I'm not hurting him, I swear. He was going to send you away, and I need you."

"Draven, please. You aren't real. None of this is real."

"If none of this is real, then you'll be opening your eyes in a mental hospital soon enough. If none of this is real, dance along in this adventure for fun. Okay?" He smiles a creepy smile. I grab my bag and bolt toward the office door, leaving before Schultz's assistant can even ask for payment.

I get a block away before Draven is at my side again.

"I didn't hurt him," he swears.

"What are you doing here?" I ask, crying. "This is a big deal for me, Draven. You've lived in Hell for five millennia, and I've only been living in Hell for a week. You have no idea how hard it was to see all of that played back to me. I needed to talk to someone!"

Draven shrugs. "I wish you would've told me. I wish you didn't keep it a secret. I could've sat with you and coached you, and made sure he didn't send you away."

"Maybe I *need* to go away." I stop in the middle of the sidewalk, tears in my eyes as I look up at Draven. "Maybe I *am* insane."

Draven sighs, shifting his weight from one foot to the other. "Okay, if that's true, and you admitted to that man that you were seeing things and hearing things, what did you think would happen?"

"He'd send me away. To a hospital. Where I could get better."

"So, then you'll wake up there. If this is all a nightmare, then just let it play out."

I shake my head. "It cannot be that simple, Draven."

Draven sighs again. "He'll only be knocked out for another hour or two—"

"Knocked out?!"

"You told him you were hearing and seeing things, and then you left. He's going to open his eyes and only remember that you were there and then gone. He's going to call your parents. The police, even. So, we have to go to the forest and do this now."

"What?"

"Now. Then you can go to the hospital, and they'll tell you that this was all a delusion or whatever. Okay? Then you'll never have to see me again."

I frown. So, that's it? Then we'll be over? I'll never see Draven again? I thought he loved me. I shake my head.

"Whatever, Draven. Take me to the stupid forest."

He grabs my hand and yanks me so hard that I worry my shoulder is going to pop out of the socket. I'm not much of an athlete, not a runner by any means, but we spring through the streets and toward the woods.

Now *these* woods, I've never been in. They're off the highway. An easy place to kill someone and hide their body, if that's what Draven plans to do.

This time, he pulls me toward a small creek that

runs over sharp, jagged rocks. I see a sewage tunnel down the current, and the water looks mossy, murky, gross. He steps into the water and pulls me in. My shoes are soaked! I can smell the sewage!

He crouches down, pulling my hand. Then I knock.

I'm in the squishy room again. I take a deep breath and shift myself, trying to find my balance and looking for the mirror. It's behind me.

Luckily, the first part goes by fast. I've seen it before. I haven't *stopped* seeing it. And then I see the rest. I see my face as I kill a man. I see, I hear, I smell, I *feel* the last moments of Brick's life.

"We're in!" Draven smiles.

He is inches away from an evil laugh. The walls begin to come toward us, the ceiling and floor closing together like magnets. Draven grabs my hand. We are submerged in this squishy jelly, and I feel all the breath, all the life, leave my body.

I can't see a thing! I can't hear a thing! I can only feel things around me. I feel elbows. I feel mouths. I feel other parts of bodies. And I feel hands grabbing at me, getting tangled in my hair. I am trapped in a pile of bodies.

Draven squeezes tighter, pulling me through them, and I try to keep my mouth shut. I feel things crawling in every crevice. My ears, my nose, my navel, under my shirt, up my skirt. I want to scream, but I also don't want to give anything the opportunity to get inside my throat.

"Draven! You came for us!" The small child's voice is right in front of me. "Who is *she*?"

I realize now that I couldn't see a thing because I had my eyes squeezed tightly shut. I open them now.

I'm standing in a room that looks like the inside of a sunset. Everything is red and orange; everything is light and heat. There is a little girl, with long black nails like Draven used to have. Another woman is standing there, long matted hair, eyes filled with black, and nails so long that they curl.

"Who is she?" the taller woman asks.

"Chosen One," Draven says quickly, grabbing both of them by the hand. He puts the little girl up onto his back and pulls the tall woman in closer. "No time to explain. Be quiet as we walk through the portal. Don't say a word."

"Hi!" the little girl greets me. The more I look at her, the more terrifying she is. She reminds me of CeCe, but only at first. The height, the pigtails. But this one has no lips. She only has sharp teeth, no nose, and huge eyes like an owl.

"Hi," I say back, and as soon as I open my mouth, I absorb a taste so foul that I fear I might puke.

"Don't," Draven says to me, grabbing my other hand. He begins to pull us, running faster than when we ran toward the portal, and I shut my eyes again, praying that he will guide me. Praying that if he really doesn't love me, he'll at least not leave me down here.

"Follow them! Follow them! Follow them!" I hear

voices repeat as we move through the crowd of bodies again.

"Get away from us!" the tall woman screams.

"Come with us! We're going to Earth," the little girl cheers. "We will get our revenge. Come with us! Come with us! Come with us!"

And I'm too terrified to say a single word.

"Knock, Bella! Knock!" Draven is screaming at the top of his lungs, and only now do I realize that I had also blocked out the noises of the bodies the first time through. All I hear are moans of pain, shrieks, screams, curses. Draven squeezes my hand, and I reach my hand out, looking for something to knock on. "Open your eyes!"

I do. All around me are bodies, bruised and bloody, faces in horror, jaws slack, eyes gouged, mouths cut open. There are hands grabbing onto my legs, hanging onto my elbows, and holding onto strands of my hair. And then, finally, over my shoulder, I see a river rock. I knock.

And just like Heaven, I hear the sounds of birds chirping and the creek moving over the rocks. I see the sunlight. I feel the California air. But most terrifying of all, I feel weightless as the dozens of bodies who held onto me, pulled me down into the pile, are now running at the speed of light away from the creek.

"Some got out—" I begin to say, but I can already tell that Draven doesn't care.

He's hugging his mother, kissing her head, crying at her feet. She doesn't look the same as she did in the

Underworld. Here, she looks like a normal woman. A mom. She's wearing a button-down dress made from old cotton material. Her hair is long and curly down her back. Her eyes are blue.

But the little girl looks the same. I scream.

She tilts her head, smiling with her terrifying mouth. "That's not very nice. I thought humans are supposed to be good. Maybe *they* should be in Hell instead."

She reaches a hand toward me, her claws becoming longer.

"Stop it, Melanesia," Draven says, and she does. "She's from a chosen family. You cannot send her to Hell, but she can sure send you back.

"Oh, no," Melanesia smiles wider, "she cannot send me back. I am half human. I am half her. I am half true demon. I am half you. She cannot send me back."

"Am I done?!" I look at Draven, stomping my feet. "Have you gotten your use out of me?"

He rolls his eyes. "Dramatic, Bella. You are being dramatic. But yes, you are done. You have gotten your use out of me, evidently, so I have gotten my use out of you."

He turns back to his mother, kissing her hands and apologizing profusely. But the mother continues to stare at me.

"Humans are disgusting," she spits.

So, no thank-yous are in order, I suppose?

"What about those things that escaped, Draven?"

"You don't have to worry about that," Melanesia

says, reaching her hand out to me. "Will you show me what a human looks like?"

I pull my hand away. "No."

"Humans are supposed to be good," she sings.

"Bye, Draven," I ignore her and say to him. He doesn't even look at me. I grab my backpack, take one last look at the family, and run away. I don't know where home is, but one way or another, I'm going to find it.

CHAPTER 8
DAVEN PORTER'S POV

Bella's father hangs up the phone as her mother paces back and forth.

"Well," he says, "that was a psychologist named Dr. Shultz—"

"Schultz," I correct. "I know him. I suggested that she go to him."

Her mother frowns, turning toward her husband. "So, she's going to therapy without telling us, too?

Secret boyfriends, secret psychologists? What else is she hiding?"

"Listen," Mr. Nova grabs his wife by the shoulders so that she'll stop pacing, "she left his office just a few hours ago. He had a fit. He thinks he passed out or had a seizure, and Bella just *left him there.*"

"She was probably having flashbacks from—" Mrs. Nova looks over at me, and then back at Mr. Nova. "You know."

"Well, she told him she was having auditory and visual hallucinations. He was just getting ready to call us, ready to call an ambulance. He highly recommends that we institutionalize her for a little bit, at least for the time being until she feels better."

"Auditory hallucinations? Visual hallucinations?" Again, Mrs. Nova looks away from her husband, then back at me, then back at her husband. "Can I talk to you in the other room, dear?"

I get the hint.

"I'm about to head home," I tell them. "I just thought you all should know that this Draven guy is... not good. He's not good at all. I can't really explain to you how not good he is. And Bella has been seeing him, and I'm scared, and I have... I feel like I'm going crazy. And I just thought you guys could help. I'm worried for her."

Mrs. Nova squints her eyes and tightens her lips together in a flat line. "What did you see, Daven?"

"What?" I ask, my voice a little shaky. I don't know *what* I saw. I'm confused about what I saw, of course.

Maybe I saw him having a video call with his sister, and the run-in with the car just jumbled all of my memories. What I thought I saw is much stranger than what makes sense. I trace the stitch above my eyebrow that I got at urgent care.

"You saw something," Mrs. Nova says, coming toward where I'm sitting at their breakfast bar. "Tell me what you saw."

"I don't know what I saw." I shrug, "I can't be sure. I hit my head pretty bad when I collided with the car."

But she just shakes her head. "I don't care if you sound crazy, Daven. Tell me what you think you saw."

I sigh.

"I think I saw Draven talking to his little sister or something."

"How?"

I let out a bigger sigh. "Via... creek water."

"Oh, God," Mr. Nova puts his hand on his chest, "you don't think..."

"And what did they talk about?" Mrs. Nova puts her hand out in front of her husband's face, indicating that he needs to shut his mouth.

"Hell," I whisper.

"Hell?"

"I think Hell," I repeat, "or the Underworld. I'm sorry, Mrs. Nova. I'm just tired, and my mom is freaking out about the concussion, and I feel like I was just having weird dreams—"

"Give him a ride," Mrs. Nova demands her husband, "and start looking for—"

"Mom?" Someone's calling from the outside. The front door swings open, and here comes Bella, out of breath, eyes swollen with tears again. "Daven?"

"Bella!" I stand up, arms outstretched as I move toward her. She flinches away.

"Take him home, *now*," Mrs. Nova repeats.

Bella's father grabs his car keys and gives his daughter a kiss on the head before heading toward the front door. I follow. Bella won't even look at me.

"Bella, I know you're mad at me," I whisper to her, "but all of this will make sense at school tomorrow. I got Stephanie to admit what she did, and they'll probably suspend her and—"

Bella finally looks at me, eyes wide, and she's about to say something when Mrs. Nova takes her under her arm and begins to lead her away. "Sorry, Daven. We have bigger things to worry about."

CHAPTER 9
BELLA NOVA'S POV

"I'VE HAD A LONG DAY," I TELL HER, FALLING ONTO my bed and folding my arms. I realize now that I've lost one of my nails. I'm upset that I'm even upset about this.

"Yeah, sounds like it," my mom says sarcastically. She sits next to me and folds her arms, too. "So, tell me about your demon boyfriend."

I roll my eyes. "What? Did Dr. Schultz call?"

It's then that I realize I'd never told Schultz about

the demon being my boyfriend. I snap my head to look at my mother. She is giving me an all-knowing look.

"Yeah, I know everything. I know more than you even think I could know. Guess how much I know, and know that I know double that."

"Okay," I unfold my arms, "then tell me what you know. Did you know that I'm the Chosen One?"

She rolls her eyes. "Less of *the* Chosen One, and more of *one* of the chosen ones."

"Why didn't you tell me?"

She sighs, unfolding her arms now. She gets down onto the floor, onto her knees. She looks up at me from there, resting her head on her arms. "I wanted you to have a normal life."

"Pretty normal!" I throw my hands up in the air. "I kill a man before I can even drive, force you all to move to a different state, date a demon—"

"Considering that all the women before you have had run-ins with death, demons, and more... it's as normal as I would've hoped." She smiles, then frowns. "I wonder if I should've told you more. About what it means to be a chosen one. There are a few families in this town who are descendants of chosen ones. But they all... well, I wouldn't say they were *lucky*. But most of them had a kid or two, all boys, and felt themselves blessed. Having a girl is the trouble."

"Great," I roll my eyes, "so I was born a mistake, too?"

My mom shakes her head. "Of course not. You are no mistake, Bella. Women descendants have the gift, which is terrifying in its own right. But the sons take more after their fathers, who don't."

I pause.

"What would you have told me, then? If you *did* decide to tell me?"

My mom crosses her fingers and closes her eyes. "That you are a mirror, Bella. Whatever you feel, people around you will reflect. The boys you fall in love with fall so hard for you because you fall so hard for them. And I'd tell you that... you'll attract demons. You'll attract bad people your whole life, my love, and you have to be stronger than them. And I'd tell you... that you should always wear a perfume that makes you happy, and whatever clothes make you feel best, and that you should do what you love and be with who you love so you can live your happiest life because, that way, all you'll do is attract happiness."

I give her a half smile. "Sounds like what any mom would tell her daughter."

She nods. "Except the mirror part, I hope."

"I guess I should've seen that on my own." I wipe a tear from my eye. "I'm sorry for being mad at you, Mom. You guys sacrificed so much to move here for me."

She gives me a full smile now.

"I was happy to move back here, Bella. Once I knew you weren't safe there, I was happy to move back here. It really is safer in this town. I know four elderly women in this town who never had children. They are descendants of chosen ones, and they still practice daily. There are three women my age, who were in my coven when I was a child—"

"You were in a coven?"

My mom sighs.

"You know, Bella. The layers between Heaven and Hell and Earth are all very thin. At any given moment, there are demons beating against the floor of Earth just waiting to get in. There are women doing the thankless jobs of keeping those demons at bay while battling the demons up here—the *humans* up here, too."

I gulp. Mom says she knows everything, times two. Does she know that I carried up ten, maybe fifteen, demons when I came back from Hell? Does she know that I was there? I'm not angry with her anymore, but I'm fearful. I'm fearful for the disappointment, the pain that's coming.

"I didn't know," I simply say, looking down at my hands that were sitting on my lap.

"Daven is in a descendant family," my mom tells me.

My head snaps up, eyes wide. "He is?"

"Yes," my mom nods, "Jackie was in my coven. We were close friends. She called me as soon as she met you. I knew you were lying about where you were, but I knew you were safe, too. The iron fences. The pentagrams. You may not have seen them, but Jackie runs a tight ship."

"Does Daven know?"

My mom shakes her head. "I don't think so."

"Huh," I mutter, "small world."

"Small world, maybe. But the Underworld is large, and the skyscraper that is Heaven is even bigger—"

"I know," I interrupt her. And I say it quickly with no other context, fearing her questions.

"You know?" she asks.

"I know."

"Know what?"

"How large the Underworld is."

Mom gets up off the floor.

"How do you know that?" She looks down at my hand. "Where's my ring?"

I put my face in my hands. "He took it."

"*Who* took it?"

"Draven?"

"Daven?"

"No!" I cry out, removing my hands and putting them at my sides. "The demon. Draven."

My mom puts her hand to her mouth. "That was the last one we had. You lost the amulet when you were younger—"

"The amulet?"

"That was the only thing that could stop an invasion, and you *lost* it, so they forged you that ring so you'd never be tempted through the Gates of Hell and—"

"How was I supposed to know?"

"I told you to never take it off!" she screams. "Why didn't you listen?"

My mother has never been this angry with me before. Her face is beet red, and she is inches from my face. Suddenly, we hear a scream coming from outside.

"What was that?" I ask.

"Oh, God!" She puts her hand to her mouth. "What did you do, Bella?"

CHAPTER 10
DRAVEN ASMODEUS' POV

"I'm terribly sorry that this must be the way we meet." I hold my hand out to Bella's mother, and she pulls her hand behind her back.

"What did you do to my daughter?" she demands.

"He didn't do anything that she didn't want to do," my own mother replies. She crosses her arms and sits on the bed. "Listen, mother to mother, let's have a talk."

Bella's mother opens her eyes wide, and she tightens her lips. "Who are you?"

"Draven, I think you should go," Bella says. Her lips are quivering.

I do as she requests. I feel the love that I have for her pouring from my heart. I can almost see her face change, see her body reacting to this love. She feels it, too.

I can feel her mother glaring at me, her eyes burning the back of my head. I flip around.

"Bella," she says, "he's manipulating your feelings. You must resist."

Bella shrinks away, jumping onto her bed. She shoves her head against her pillow.

"Listen," my mother says, "my son made a mistake long ago. He has corrected that mistake today, but now my husband—"

"My step-father is a very powerful demon," I jump in, cutting my mother off. "He wants her and my half-sister back. Bella accidentally let out a few demons when we saved my mother and sister, and those demons brought with them some of her essence, and they have opened the portal."

"I have to make some calls." Mrs. Nova begins to head out of the room. "Draven, you come with me."

"No," I state, "I need you all to come with *me*. The demons are escaping Hell at an alarming rate. Things are bad, and I acknowledge that most of this is my fault. I think Bella will be highly sought after, and we need to keep her safe somewhere. I should carry her down to Hell—"

"Ha!" her mother snorts. "Fat chance, buddy. We can handle this up here."

"Listen," my own mother shakes her head. "Bella isn't safe here. My husband knows that she helped release me. He is going to be looking for her. You all need to find somewhere safe to stay."

"Give her the ring back." Bella's mother looks at me, ignoring my mother. I dig it out of my back pocket and hand it back to Bella, who sobs.

"Lucifer's army is rising. With all due respect, we need to get you all somewhere safe."

"I will *never* step through the Gates of Hell *again*," her mother repeats. "Bella, put this on. It'll help you resist him."

Her mother digs in the closet, pulling out a yellow shawl. It's hard for me to look at Bella as she wraps herself in it.

"Look." I start to speak louder, turning to her mother. "I did some bad things. I am a demon. I spent so much time in the Underworld that I don't know left from right, and I do crave blood. I do crave torture. I do crave destruction. But I have resisted every urge because your daughter is special, and I love her, and—"

"Stop!" Mrs. Nova puts her hand up. "Stop right now."

"No!" I shout, and my eyes fill with fire. "She is in grave danger. Swallow your pride and—"

"This may come as a shock," she continues, "but

we have been doing just fine up here without double agents. Bella will be safe here because I'm here, and because there are dozens of women on this land who are probably already fighting the army off, and—"

"No." My mother shakes her head and stands up, going toward Bella's mother. Bella's mother steps away. "I was never meant to go to Hell. I was a good mother. I was a good person. My son made an awful choice, took my *other* son from me, and... it was like I didn't belong on Earth anymore because it brought too much pain."

"He did what?" Bella sits up on her bed. I feel a coldness all over my body. I *did* tell her that demons lie, after all. I did.

"My son made mistakes, but he is righting them. I had no doubt that he'd free us, but I thought it would end in death and destruction for your kind. Your daughter changed him. She changed his heart. Believe me, he wants to help you."

"Demons lie," her mother says quickly. Bella nods.

"I am no demon. I am a mother," my mother reaches out her hand. "I am truly good. I am."

I see Mrs. Nova considering it.

"Please, just go," she says. "You'll want to leave, trust me. I'm going to fill the entire house with the essence of lemon, and you are going to feel like you're choking. *Go.*"

CHAPTER 11
BELLA NOVA'S POV

"Mom," I repeat. She is drawing pentagrams up and down my arm. I can hear the screams from the streets, and I smell ash. "Are you sure we're safe here?"

"I have been preparing for this my whole life," my mother says. She pulls out a pair of my pajamas and puts them on my lap. "Go take an Epsom salt bath. Rub the rocks into your skin. Then dress. You need rest. It's harder for them to possess you if you are asleep."

"Mom, please let me help," I plead, pushing the pajamas back. She shakes her head.

"I need to make some calls."

"I'm sorry, Mom!" I plead again.

She gives me a soft smile but pulls out her phone. I see my dad's picture pop up across the phone screen. She answers, and I can hear more screaming. She frowns, like she's about to cry, and then leaves my room, shutting the door behind me. I hear scraping against the floor. When I go to my door and try to push it gently, it won't budge.

She blocked me in!

I let out a breath and tap my foot.

If I really am the Chosen One, I cannot be stopped by a locked door!

I squeeze my eyes shut and think of Draven. I think of when I first met him, and our first time together, and our first kiss. And poof! Just like magic, here he is, sitting on my bed.

"Your mother is just about as stubborn as mine," he says.

He has a coy side smile, even though the world is crumbling outside. It's unfortunate that it still makes my heart skip a beat. It's clear as day just how awful he's been to me these past few days. But wouldn't I do the same for my mother? She certainly did the same for me.

"Draven," is all I can manage to say.

He stands up, closing the distance between us.

"I'm sorry for how I acted today, Bella. But I was

stressed about this, okay? I needed to get my mother up here, and I needed to get my sister up here, and I don't even know where she is now—"

"I get it," I cut him off. "I wouldn't do the same thing for Ace, necessarily. But I'd do the same for my mother. And she did, basically, do the same thing for me. But why did you lie about all of this?"

"It felt like it was worth the risk for me," he says, shrugging, "but I'm sorry."

I nod. "Am I safe here?"

"Probably not."

I sigh.

"My mother told me to take a salt bath."

"That's probably a good idea. That and lemon repulse demons. No one will grab onto you when I take you down there," he replies. "I'll wait here."

My eyes widen, and I shake my head. "No, no, no. I'm not going down there with you—"

"He will never look for you down in Hell."

"But it's *Hell!*"

"So, take a nap. Many are being dragged to Hell right now by the demons, anyway. You'd probably be dragged down there eventually, too. Maybe we can disguise you. You'd hope for Hell if you knew what my step-father would do to either of us if he finds us here."

"No," I shake my head, "I won't."

"Not a choice, Princess," he tells me.

"What? You're going to kidnap me?"

He sighs. "I'd rather not, Bella. I'd rather you come with me willingly."

I rub my forehead with my thumb and forefinger. I want to cry again.

Without another word, I go toward the bathroom. My mom has run the bath and filled it with lemon-scented Epsom salts. I undress, get in the tub, and rub the salt all over my body. What will I do? Is this all my fault? Why didn't I... couldn't I have... shouldn't I have...? I feel sick. I might puke. I scroll through my phone out of bad habit. There are hundreds of messages from Daven.

All I see are newscasts of Hell on Earth... at least, in our little town. I see Daven's father, the mayor, handing out shotguns at the Capitol. I see people being dragged under water, dragged into trees. I see blood running through the streets.

I lean over the side of the tub and puke.

When I finally managed to rub the salt into every crevice of my body, I put on the pair of pajamas that my mom gave me. They smell like laundry detergent, like home, like her. And it's all my fault that this will all be gone within a matter of days, maybe hours.

When I leave the bathroom, Draven is lying on my bed.

"I'll go with you if we can release everyone from Hell."

"What?" Draven sits up. "How?"

"I released your mother, didn't I? I can release everyone who is being dragged down there. I can release the people who were wrongfully taken, and—"

"It's going to be a game you never win. As long as

there are demons roaming Earth, you'll have to keep on releasing people over and over and over—"

"Whatever! I'll sacrifice myself. I'll make it my life's work to lead people out of the Underworld. I *am* a chosen one. This is my fault; this is my doing. I will spend an eternity correcting my mistakes. I will spend an eternity underground in torture to fix this mistake."

"Wow," Draven shakes his head, "you really are a good person. You are much better than me, and much too good for me."

"Prove me wrong," I say to him. "Help me do it."

CHAPTER 12
CECE PORTER'S POV

I don't understand what's going on, but I know everyone on TV looks scared. Everyone except mama.

She pulls me up the stairs. I'm wearing my new yellow raincoat that Daven gave to me from Bella. When he got home, mom and dad took him to bed because he got hit by a car today. That would've been the weirdest part of my day if it's not currently raining tar, if cars aren't being abandoned on the streets, if I couldn't hear the screams of the city from inside our gated home.

If I didn't know that demons are roaming the streets.

"How do you know that?" mama asks. She gives me a necklace that's decorated with pentagrams. It has one large crystal, called selenite, hanging down from the center. I put it around my neck.

"I just have a feeling," I reply. And I do. As soon as the tar began raining down, it was as sure as seeing a nest with eggs in it. Those are going to be baby birds—there are demons roaming the streets.

My mama smiles. "Your powers are strong, my love."

"Will they get us?" I ask.

She shakes her head. "Our gates are made of iron. They will never get through."

"Is the world over?"

"Not if I can help it."

Mama kisses me on the forehead and picks me up. She hasn't picked me up like this in a long time. She stands tall and strong and confident, though I'm sure there is a worry deep inside of her. But if there really is a worry, she refuses to let me know. She never does. With her, I am stronger because she is strong.

She takes me down a long hallway and brings me toward a closet. It's always been locked. Mama said her wedding China is in there. So, I don't care about it being locked, not until now. Not until she unlocks it, and I see an entire room in there. It's made of iron, with beautiful sparkling pentagrams drawn across the floor and the ceiling, with salt lining all the walls and no windows.

"What is this?" I ask.

"You stay in here, okay? I'm going to go get your brother. You will both stay in here until this all blows over."

I shake my head quickly, my pigtails bouncing. "Where will you go? Can I go with you? Where is papa?"

"He's fixing this the only way he knows how. Luckily, I know a better way."

"Can I please go with you?"

"Afraid not, sweetie." She pushes me through the door and closes it behind me.

I sigh, going toward a velvety chair near the wall. When I sit down, I feel something poke my butt. There is something sharp in the pocket of this coat. Another gift from Bella?

I pull out a large golden pentagram on a string, beaded with gorgeous crystal beads. It begins to glow in my hands.

"I better bring this to mama. This will help," I whisper to myself, easily pushing the door open and going to find her.

CHAPTER 13
BELLA NOVA'S POV

Hell wasn't packed before.

There is nothing compared to this.

When we enter Hell again, something new plays on the mirror. It's not my murder of Brick. This time, it's of me having sex with Draven. It's our relationship that plays back. He's sad next to me as he watches my greatest sin, *him*.

But I don't care anymore. I'm done with love, and

I'm done with Earthly things. I am sacrificing myself. I will help others escape from Hell.

After I view my greatest sin, I am nearly suffocated with the compaction of other humans. They are crying, asking where they are, screaming.

"How do I know who's a demon and who's human?" I ask Draven. As I open my mouth, elbows and fingers touch my tongue.

"They're all demons now."

"How am I to know who is good, and who can be released?"

"Bella!" he screams to me over the yelling. "You *won't* know. It'll be hard to know."

I encourage the people to grab onto me, first going for those I already recognize… which just happens to be Stephanie and her minions. Stephanie cries, sobs, screams, eyes bleeding as she grabs onto my neck like a child getting a piggyback ride. She is the first person I save.

"Go hide. Rub your body with Epsom salt. Draw a pentagram on yourself. Find something that smells like lemon, wear bright clothes, do what you can to think happy thoughts," I say to her. She's still crying, listening only long enough to hear the full speech, then takes off running, tripping over herself in the distance.

It's exhausting watching Draven and I over and over again, our entire relationship playing on a mirror as I go back and forth in between Hell and Earth. It's torture for Draven, too, and we take turns playing our greatest sins in the mirror for entrance into Hell as we go back and forth.

His first few times is an image of him sacrificing his own twin brother in order to meet Lucifer, to have food and money. As he watches our relationship through my eyes more, his sin eventually changes. He, too, watches the abuse that he'd put me through.

It's like feeling the pain of a breakup that should've never been a relationship in the first place, and it's agony. But if I have to spend an eternity doing this, maybe it's what I deserve.

Our fifteenth time down, Draven stops me before I go back up.

"My sister is calling for me," he says. But I don't hear anything.

"Yeah, right," I huff, someone's hair filling my mouth. "You're just sick of this. You're just being a coward."

"Come with me!" He pulls me by the hand before I can say anything else.

We move quietly through the crowd of bodies, and I see the route that he had taken me when we first saved his mother and sister. Past the bodies, there are walls of fire, and the ceiling is made of tar. He pulls it down over us, and instead of being in the tar like I had expected, we're in the empty sunset room.

On the wall of the sunset room, his sister—looking much more human-like—appears.

"I have the amulet," she says.

Draven sighs. "Great. So, that's the end, right? Of the human race?"

She shakes her head. "I have made a friend."

Behind his sister, I can make out a pair of familiar pigtails.

"CeCe?" I whisper.

"The amulet will stop the war," his sister says, "and send all the demons back to Hell, bring the dead back to life, reverse it all, and erase their memories."

"So, what are you going to do? Destroy it?"

She shakes her head. "I like it here. And I like my new friend."

"Hi, Bella!" CeCe waves. "I like your pajamas!"

I look down at my pajamas, now covered in dirt and blood.

"CeCe?" I cry out. "Are you safe?"

"I don't like her," his sister huffs. "She's hysterical. We should leave her in Hell."

"No!" CeCe yells. "I love Bella. Bring her back up here."

"I'm letting you keep the amulet and send all the demons back to Hell," Melanesia responds, turning to CeCe. "I desire one thing, and it is for her to stay down there."

My heart stops. I feel the breath leave my lungs, like it has already been decided.

If this is what I deserve, then fine.

"No," Draven interjects, "let me stay down here in her place."

"You?" His sister laughs. "My father will torture you forever. For eternity!"

Draven looks over at me, and tears fall down his face. "I will sacrifice myself. This is all my fault."

"But you just got your mother back!" I shake my head. "You just got your sister back."

He falls to his knees. "I am a monster, Bella. This is all my fault. It was my fault that she was even down here in the first place."

"Mother will want you back." Melanesia has a mischievous smile pressed across her face.

"Mother hates me," Draven mumbles. "She will want her son. She will want the son I killed. Bring him back, Melanesia. She will be happy."

"Hmm," she sings. Then she shrugs. "Okay."

"Draven, thank you—" I reach out to hold him, and he is on his knees, crying, fearful, frantic, and suddenly, I am at the creek again. The water is running over my bare feet.

CHAPTER 14
DAVEN PORTER'S POV

I don't remember anything after the car accident. I have some stitches on my head and some bruises on my ribs, but that's all. Bella comes over to my house, but not to see me. She tells me that Draven is gone, and she's almost sad about it.

And I must have a concussion because as the women whisper in the kitchen, it sounds like *CeCe* is the reason that Draven is gone.

"Your mother said the authorities might be on their

way," my mother says to Bella. "She asked me to keep you safe."

Bella sighs. "Daven, can you please give us a moment alone?"

I nod, going toward the kitchen door. But I still press my head against it and hear my mother say, "So you killed him, Bella? But he was possessed, right? And a bad man, wasn't he—Cliff!"

My dad comes down the stairs, and he also looks shaken. He looks a bit bruised, a little pale.

"Get away from that door," he says sternly. I do. I go into the living room, watching them from the frosted glass that separates the two rooms.

I can see them, blurrily, as I sit on the couch, grasping for words that they are saying. My dad comes out of the kitchen quickly and goes toward his office, and I hear Bella speaking.

"The guilt was killing me," she says, "and after everything that's happened—"

And then her voice gets quiet again. This sucks, and I'm done waiting to speak to her.

I go toward the kitchen and open the door.

"CeCe," Bella crouches down, putting her hands out toward my baby sister, "it seems I have a lot to thank you for today."

She whispers, "I saw him before. In my dreams."

"Nightmares," Bella corrects.

"Oh, no," CeCe says, looking at me, "dreams. I've killed him every time. It was... glorious!"

"Your mother never told you that you're a descendant, right?"

CeCe shakes her head.

"A descendant?" I ask. They ignore me.

"Well, I don't think I can get away from telling her," my mother chimes in.

Bella smiles, then hesitates, blushing before she asks, "Did you know right away when you met me?"

"You look just like your mother. If I had seen her in town, or known she had moved back, I'd have recognized her right away."

"I guess being a shut-in has some benefits," Bella laughs, giving a side smile, "or maybe it doesn't. Maybe this whole thing could've been avoided."

"Things always go how they should. Life isn't a fairytale, Bella." My mother winks. "Go get some rest. You two have a lot to catch up on." She then looks over at me.

Bella smiles and looks at my sister, crouching down to whisper in her ear as my mother turns on her heels to the screaming tea kettle. I can just barely hear Bella whisper, "Be careful about your new friend. Do you have the—"

And then CeCe holds up a strange golden necklace that I've never seen before.

"Trade me?" Bella asks. She gives CeCe the pentagram ring from her own finger, and Bella takes the necklace. She leaves it on the counter as my mom pours a cup of tea, and my mother puts it into her pocket quickly.

I hold my hand out to Bella, and she takes it, following me to my bedroom. When we get there, we collapse onto my bed, exhausted. Though thoughts tempt me, I'm exhausted, and I can tell she is, too.

She is wearing a pair of dirty pajamas—blue and white striped shorts and a white tank top—that she saved (or nearly ended?) the world in. There is dirt on her forehead. She has her hair, tangled and matted, in a bun at the top of her head.

"I don't think I understand what happened today." I am trying to understand what I saw, who I saw, what CeCe had to do with any of this. What my mother knows and why she knows it. All I know for certain, at this moment, is that I was right about Draven. And I'm proud of it.

"I can try to start from the beginning," she says. "Start with what happened in Oregon."

And then I remember why Bella is here in the first place, hiding out in our mansion while her family goes to find help from all corners of the world. Because there are authorities on the way, for one reason or another.

"Tell me."

"I haven't made the best decisions my whole life," she explains, tucking a strand of hair behind her ear.

If it's stupid to fall under her spell, to believe her innocence even knowing her guilt, than I am a fool. I will wear the badge with honor. I give her a kiss on the forehead and tell her I don't need any more details. I go over to my dresser, where a red bag has been waiting for her. Inside the bag is a black box. I pull out a ring, my grandmother's, from the box.

"This isn't a marriage proposal, because I think both our moms would lose their minds." I laugh. She smiles, tears filling her eyes. "But it *is* an honest promise, Bella."

She shakes her head. "I don't even know where to being, Daven. You have only been honest with me. You never faltered; you never lied. I love you, Daven, and I'm sorry for everything."

I shrug. "I could've gone about things differently, too."

She takes the ring and looks it over before putting it on her finger. "The ring of a descendant, your grandmother. Our marriage will be so blessed."

She is beaming, but then she frowns, taking the ring off her finger.

"Is there something wrong?"

She hands it back to me.

"I made some bad choices before I moved here, Daven."

I laugh. "There's nothing that could stop me from marrying you, Bella. You could've killed a man in cold blood, and I'd still love you."

Her eyes widen, and she puts her hand over her mouth. "What?"

Her voice is muffled.

"What?" I ask. I feel a little light-headed, but I think I've solved the mystery. "Did you... you didn't..."

Bella looks down at her hand, now ringless. "He

was going to hurt me, Daven. And it's complicated. It's hard to explain all these factors, but maybe one day, your mom will sit you down and—"

"I don't care."

"But if I'm arrested, if I have to go to jail... I don't think self-defense counts if you pick up and run, Daven, and I'm scared I'll have to go away—"

"No," I shake my head, "take this ring and put it on. Let me go talk to my dad—"

"Your mother has already asked him to look things over and—"

"No," I say again.

I shut the door behind me and go down the hall, toward the study.

When I look through the glass panes of his French doors, he has his reading glasses on and is peering over a paper document that's thick with length. Before I even knock, my hand hanging limp in front of the door, he motions for me to enter. I do so quietly.

"Dad, I..."

"It seems that we are harboring a fugitive," he simply says.

I can see now that the document, even with its thickness, has small letters. It seems as if a hundred paragraphs are spread across one page. When I was younger, I would be shocked with the way he reads these papers. But he always told me that it was his degree in law, his political background, that has prepared him to read these. I asked if all those in power could do what he does, and he just laughed.

He laughed because he said no one else cared enough.

"I don't think she—"

"Spare me." He puts up his hand. "I don't have time. She did it. But truth is, the man she killed was an awful man, and there's irrefutable evidence pointing to that. The biggest crime she committed wasn't the killing, but the running."

"What can you do?"

"Well," he motions toward the papers, "that is what I'm trying to figure out."

"Sir." I'm surprised to hear Bella's voice behind me. My dad looks up at her, peering just above his glasses to see her in her dirty pajamas.

"You've had quite the day, Ms. Nova," he replies. "You should be resting."

I see Bella raise an eyebrow. "You know what my day was like?"

He gives her a soft, knowing smile. "I don't remember first-hand, but my wife has filled me in on the details. It is a blessing and a curse—no, only a blessing—that you women are the only ones who will remember today. You should be *resting*. It was because you didn't rest that you made the irrational decision to confess to the crime."

"In my defense—"

"No need to defend yourself here. I think you did the right thing. It's just a matter of helping everyone else see that you did the right thing."

"And if they do, we might have a chance?"

He sighs, scratching his forehead. "Bella, why did your family run?"

She comes forward, pushing past me to sit on the chair in front of his desk. I feel invisible, as I should. Bella has seen so much. She and my father know what true pain and dedication and loyalty and sacrifice are. In this way, they are immortal. Their age isn't a number but a status, a badge they wear.

She is calm and collected, her answer clear. "If you thought Daven had done something wrong, if you were worried that bringing it into the light would be a danger to the world... wouldn't you have done the same?"

My dad thinks about this, thumb stroking his chin. "I'd love to speak to your mother and father. It must've taken a lot out of them."

"They never should've had me," she utters, and not in an angry or petty way, just a statement of fact. "But my grandmother never should've had her, and so on and so forth. They knew what our blood would bring on the day of the reckoning. But she gave birth to me and just wanted me to have a normal life. Wouldn't you just want your kids to have a normal life?"

"I do." He nods. "I always have. We went through the same thing before having Daven—I can't even tell you how many superstitions we attempted just to make sure he came out a boy. We did the same things with CeCe, and despite it all, she came out this spitfire of a girl. And thank goodness. Without her, we'd all be... well. We'll figure this out, Ms. Nova. I can make no guarantees, but I foresee my son and you having a bright future. Jail time is not in that future. Reconciliation of some sort, maybe. But not jail time."

"Thank you so much," she whispers, her voice cracking.

I'm relieved when he says it, and I can see Bella's shoulders deflate. She looks back at me, eyes widening, pleased. I am beaming at her.

"Relax, though. No wedding bells until you both graduate. Then we'll be happy to do for you what we can to make your dream wedding possible." My dad looks at me when he says this, and he winks. I look down at Bella's hand, where my grandmother's sparking ring sits in place of her pentagram ring. It looks much better, suits her so much better.

I cannot wait to put a ring on that finger and invite her to be my bride.

EPILOGUE
BELLA NOVA'S POV

Ten years later...

I CRY OUT IN THE MIDDLE OF THE NIGHT sometimes because I hear him. I cannot, and will not, explain this ever-present connection to Daven. I don't need to, I don't think.

It's possible to hate someone, and love someone, and be thankful for them, and regret ever meeting them, all at the same time. Because that is how I feel about Draven.

On nights where I am able, if I fall asleep in just the right manner, I visit him. He isn't in as much trouble as he and his sister had imagined—his sister, who is now the "godmother" of my son, all of its irony making us laugh—and his father didn't remember anything about the great war. None of the demons did. The amulet was more powerful than anyone could've imagined. And how funny then, that I had lost it for twelve years because I had taken it and put it in my pocket.

Daven and I got married on the day my case was closed. It was a case of self-defense. I was free to live my life, and I went on to open a non-profit organization to support women who have been in similar situations.

Cliff Porter found a bunch of lawyers to support my cause, to help other women who acted in self-defense be free. What the lawyers didn't know was that about one in five clients actually killed someone they had truly loved, who had been possessed by a demon. Those were the hardest cases, but those women deserved their freedom, too.

The coven community is stronger now than it was in my mother's day. I practice, with my mother and mother-in-law, during full moons, new moons, and dark moons. We tell Daven that we're just going to brunch and the mall. Melanesia and her mother even come every now and then, though her mother tries to stay away from all that stuff. She'll come around, though.

I am pregnant. Today, we find out the gender. She is a girl. She is a new descendant. And it is time that we tell Daven the truth.

UNLEASHING HELL BOOK THREE

SAVING THEM

VIOLA TEMPEST